TINGO
TANGO
MANGO
TREE

STORY BY
MARCIA VAUGHAN

PICTURES BY
YVONNE BUCHANAN

Silver Burdett Press

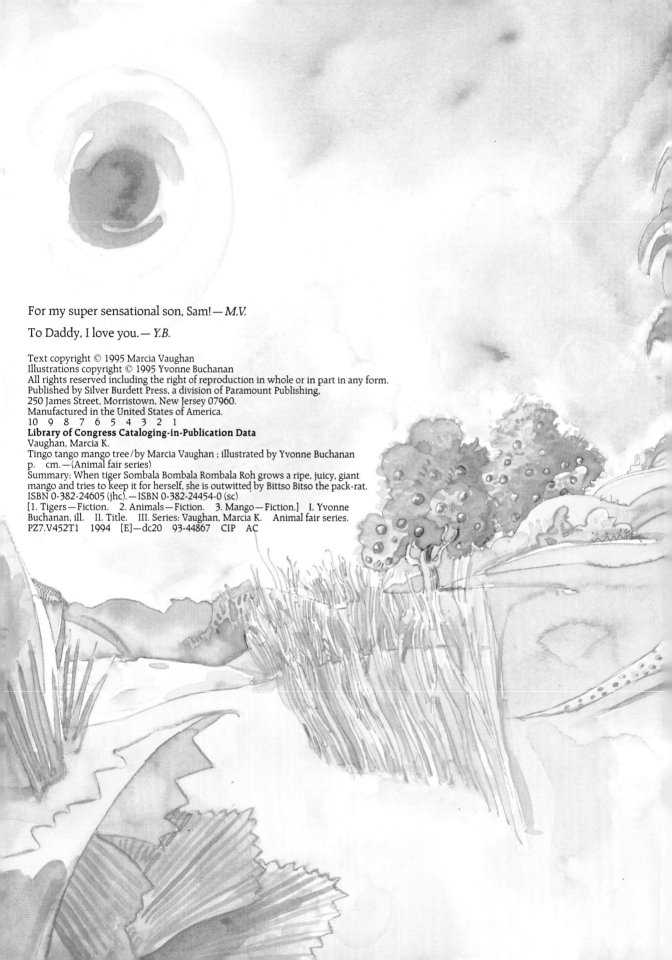

For my super sensational son, Sam! — *M.V.*

To Daddy, I love you. — *Y.B.*

Text copyright © 1995 Marcia Vaughan
Illustrations copyright © 1995 Yvonne Buchanan
All rights reserved including the right of reproduction in whole or in part in any form.
Published by Silver Burdett Press, a division of Paramount Publishing,
250 James Street, Morristown, New Jersey 07960.
Manufactured in the United States of America.
10 9 8 7 6 5 4 3 2 1
Library of Congress Cataloging-in-Publication Data
Vaughan, Marcia K.
Tingo tango mango tree / by Marcia Vaughan ; illustrated by Yvonne Buchanan
p.   cm. — (Animal fair series)
Summary: When tiger Sombala Bombala Rombala Roh grows a ripe, juicy, giant
mango and tries to keep it for herself, she is outwitted by Bittso Bitso the pack-rat.
ISBN 0-382-24605 (jhc). — ISBN 0-382-24454-0 (sc)
[1. Tigers — Fiction.   2. Animals — Fiction.   3. Mango — Fiction.]   I. Yvonne
Buchanan, ill.   II. Title.   III. Series: Vaughan, Marcia K.   Animal fair series.
PZ7.V452T1   1994   [E] — dc20   93-44867   CIP   AC

One day, as Sombala Bombala Rombala Roh, the iguana, was walking, she found a giant mango seed and secretly set out to plant it. Across the beach, past the orange grove, through the sugar cane field, and deep into the forest snuck Sombala Bombala Rombala Roh.

Whup, whup, whup. She dug a hole in the warm earth.

Pip! She plopped the mango seed in.

Pap, pap, pap. She patted the soil over the seed till it was as smooth as a palm frond.

Every day, instead of helping pull in the nets, pick the oranges, and cut the sugar cane, Sombala Bombala Rombala Roh would fill a calabash gourd with water and carry it into the forest singing,

"Tingo tango mango tree.
Grow a mango just for me.
The biggest mango that can be,
Will grow upon my mango tree."

Sweee-hooosh. Sombala Bombala Rombala Roh splashed the water over the seed and sat in the sun to wait.

Sure enough, one day up popped a mango tree. Pushing and stretching, twisting and turning, it reached up-uppity-up toward the sun-so-hot. And way up on the tip-most, top-most branch there grew and grew and grew and *grew* a big, ripe, juicy, giant mango!

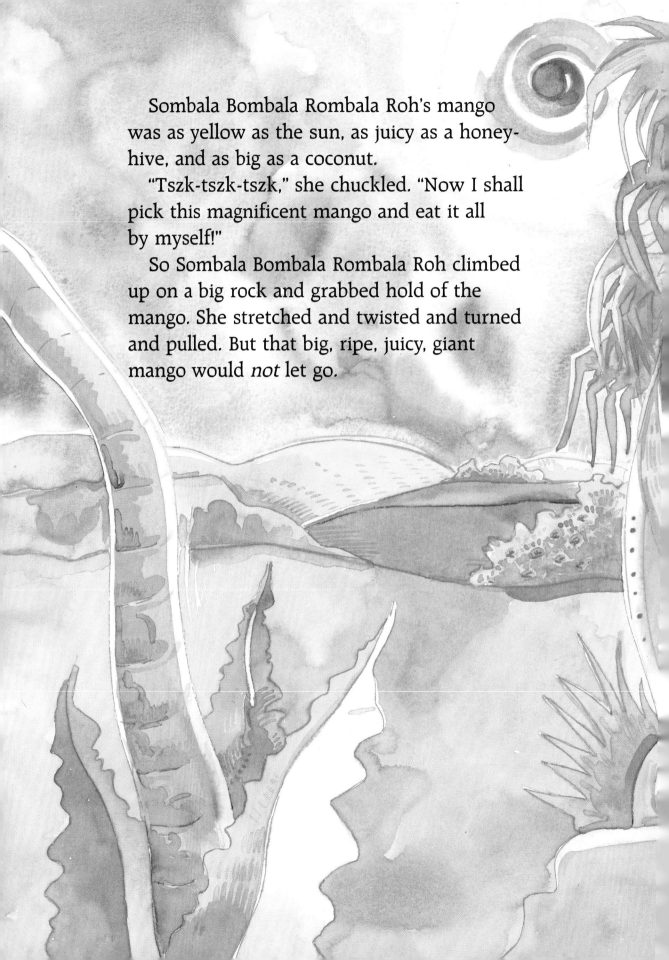

Sombala Bombala Rombala Roh's mango
was as yellow as the sun, as juicy as a honey-
hive, and as big as a coconut.

"Tszk-tszk-tszk," she chuckled. "Now I shall
pick this magnificent mango and eat it all
by myself!"

So Sombala Bombala Rombala Roh climbed
up on a big rock and grabbed hold of the
mango. She stretched and twisted and turned
and pulled. But that big, ripe, juicy, giant
mango would *not* let go.

Arumba. Arumba. Arumba. Sombala
Bombala Rombala Roh hurried to the cane
field and told Kokio Lokio Mokio Koh, the
flamingo, to follow her into the forest.

"Kokio Lokio Mokio Koh,
Help me pick my ripe mango.
If you do you'll get one bite.
Now pull and pull with all your might."

So Kokio Lokio Mokio Koh pulled.
And Sombala Bombala Rombala Roh pulled.
But that big, ripe, juicy, giant mango would
not let go.

Arumba. Arumba. Arumba. Sombala
Bombala Rombala Roh scuttled to the orange
grove and told Willaby Dillaby Dallaby Doh,
the parrot, to follow her into the forest.

"Willaby Dillaby Dallaby Doh,
Help me pick my ripe mango.
If you do you'll get one bite.
Now pull and pull with all your might."

So Willaby Dillaby Dallaby Doh pulled.
Kokio Lokio Mokio Koh pulled.
And Sombala Bombala Rombala Roh pulled.
But that big, ripe, juicy, giant mango would
not let go.

Arumba. Arumba. Arumba. Sombala
Bombala Rombala Roh scurried to the edge of
the sea and told Nanaba Panaba Tanaba Goh,
the turtle, to follow her into the forest.

"Nanaba Panaba Tanaba Goh,
Help me pick my ripe mango.
If you do you'll get one bite.
Now pull and pull with all your might."

So Nanaba Panaba Tanaba Goh pulled.
Willaby Dillaby Dallaby Doh pulled.
Kokio Lokio Mokio Koh pulled.
And Sombala Bombala Rombala Roh pulled.
But that big, ripe, juicy, giant mango would
not let go.

Just then, Bitteo Biteo, the bat, awoke and came *flit, flit, flit* through the forest. "Sombala Bombala Rombala Roh, I see that you are trying to pick that big, ripe, juicy, giant mango."

"What's it to you?" Sombala Bombala Rombala Roh snapped.

"Well now," Bitteo Biteo declared. "I can get that mango down, one, two, three."

"Hah!" the iguana sneered. "A bitty little bat like you could never pick a big, ripe, juicy, giant mango like mine. *Never!*"

So saying, she stretched out on the hot rock and fell asleep.

Pah-ree-rurr. Pah-ree-rurr. As the iguana began to snore, Bitteo Biteo flit-fluttered up the tree, landed on the tip-most, top-most branch, and bit the mango stem, one, two, three.

Down plunged the mango, *whap-smack* on top of Sombala Bombala Rombala Roh's head. There it broke into four big, ripe, juicy, giant pieces.

And Kokio Lokio Mokio Koh, Willaby Dillaby Dallaby Doh, Nanaba Panaba Tanaba Goh, and Bitteo Biteo ate it all up, don't you know!

Later, when Sombala Bombala Rombala Roh
awoke, all she found of her big, ripe, juicy,
giant mango...was the seed.

"Tin - go tan - go man - go tree,

Grow a man - go just for me. The

big - gest man - go that can be will

grow up - on my man - go tree."

Pronunciation Guide:
Sombala Bombala Rombala Roh: SOHM-bah-lah BOHM-bah-lah ROHM-bah-lah Roh
Kokio Lokio Mokio Koh: KOH-kee-oh LOH-kee-oh MOH-kee-oh Koh
Willaby Dillaby Dallaby Doh: WILL-ah-be DILL-ah-be DAL-ah-be Doh
Nanaba Panaba Tanaba Goh: NAN-ah-bah PAN-ah-bah TAN-ah-bah Goh
Bitteo Biteo: BIT-ee-oh BITE-ee-oh